Blame It On The Rum

On The Rocks

Shaw Hart

 Created with Vellum

Want a free book?

You can grab Sweets **Here.**
Check out my website, www.shawhart.com for
more free books!

*

He's the worst best thing that's ever happened to me.

Walking around with Hayes Montrose is like walking around with an angry thundercloud hovering above your head.

He's too big, too grumpy, and entirely too attractive.

So, what's he doing with a frumpy wallflower like me?

I have no idea and he won't tell me.

All I do know is that it started five days ago when I walked into the bar that he works at and he's been glued to my side ever since.

I should be annoyed by his bossy attitude or sick of him always watching me, but the big guy is growing on me.

Until he tells me what happened the first night that we met.

Now I'm just wondering which of us is crazier.

And why being with him feels so right.

Chapter One

B etty

Well, last night was a mistake.

That's the first coherent thought that I have as I wake up in a stranger's bed the day after with my head pounding and my mouth tasting like I licked the bottom of a garbage can. I search my brain, trying to remember what happened, where I am, and how I ended up here, but it's all just a kaleidoscope of random images and sounds.

I wince as I roll over and when my stomach threatens to revolt, I give up and lie back down on my back. I have to close my eyes because it feels like the room is spinning and I decide right then and there that I am never drinking again. This is all the rum's fault.

After a few minutes, I try again. I need to get out of there before whoever's bed I'm in comes back.

"Ugh," I groan as I move to sit up, pushing my wild red hair out of my eyes.

I look around the room. Thankfully I'm the only one here and it looks like the other side of the bed is undisturbed, so chances are that I slept alone too. I'm still wearing my clothes too, and I let out a sigh. It would suck to not remember losing my virginity.

The room is pretty bare, just a bed and dresser. There are no mementos on the wall, just a gorgeous painting of a sunset on the wall by the door leading to the bathroom. I wonder if they just moved in. Whoever they are.

I climb out of bed and pad over to the bathroom. It's obviously a man's place, judging by the lack of feminine products or touches. A razor sits on the sink next to a toothbrush holder, a tube of toothpaste, and a bottle of soap.

I look even worse than I thought that I would when I stare at my reflection in the bathroom mirror. I hurry to go to the bathroom and splash some water on my face. When that does nothing, I grab the soap and wash my face again. It doesn't really help with the mascara circles under my eyes, but I at least feel a little better, a little more awake.

I need to get out of here.

My shoes and purse are on top of the dresser and I grab both of them, grateful that all of my things are together so that I can make a quick escape.

I'm wondering if I'll be able to get out of here without running into whoever's place this is when the bedroom door opens.

I squeak as I take in the huge man that comes in.

He takes up most of the doorframe and my jaw drops as I take all of him in. He's got pitch black hair that looks like it's in need of a trim. The ends curl up, giving him a slightly boyish look, but that's the only thing boylike about him.

His arms are thick, well, actually, all of him is thick, but his arms especially look like his muscles have muscles. He's wearing a plain black T-shirt that looks like it's really struggling to wrap all the way around his torso. It clings to the planes of his stomach and makes him look even more imposing.

He has a scar running across one eye, through his eyebrow, and across his forehead, where it disappears into his hair. I can't help but wonder how he got it.

My eyes trace over his lean hips and down his tree-trunk thighs and I can see why I chose to go home with him, even in my drunken stupor. He's so hot, even with the scar on the left side of his face.

"You're awake," he says, his deep voice rolling over me like smoke.

"Yep," I say, but it comes out more like a squeak.

When did my voice get so high pitched? And why do I sound so breathless? I've been lying in bed and I sound like I just ran five miles.

"I made you breakfast. And coffee. Do you need a Tylenol or anything?" he adds after a beat and I nod dumbly.

I've never been great at talking to guys. That was part of the reason why I went out last night. I'm trying to spread my wings a bit.

He comes back into the bedroom with a bottle of pain reliever pills in his hand and I gladly take it from him.

"Thanks," I say and he studies me, his bright blue eyes narrowing slightly as I grab the bottle of water that he must have left out on the end table.

I swallow down the pills and pray that they take effect soon. My eyes are drawn back to the mystery man in front of me. He's so much bigger than me, but that's not what has me unable to look away from him.

There's just something about him. He has my body feeling hotter, my blood pumping faster, and my heart racing.

I'm attracted to him.

I was starting to think that it would never happen. I never dated in high school or college. It was hard to trust people when you knew that they knew who your parents were and that they were most likely just using you to get to them or their connections.

I don't get that feeling with this guy though, and I wonder why that is.

"You don't remember me, do you," he says and even though it's a question, he doesn't make it sound like one.

"No, I'm so sorry. I drank too much last night, which was so stupid," I start to ramble, but I stop when I see the look in his eyes.

He looks... hurt.

The corners of his lips dip down, and he shifts on those enormous feet of his.

"Thank you for taking care of me last night. I mean, I can't really remember it, but I'm assuming that it was you who tucked me in and stuff."

He just nods once and I bite my bottom lip.

Should I stop talking? Should I just make a run for the door? What's proper one-night stand etiquette? Does that even apply here? We didn't actually sleep together.

"I'll be in the kitchen," he says and then he turns and heads back out of the bedroom.

I frown after him, wondering if I said something wrong. I need coffee. Then I'll be able to think clearly.

I follow him into the kitchen. His cabin is kind of small,

just a kitchen, bedroom, and living room, but it's nice. Tidy. I feel relaxed here and that should be strange. I don't know this guy, so shouldn't I be worried about being alone with him?

I guess something in my gut tells me he's alright. An image of him helping me off of my stool last night, his hands careful and gentle as they cupped my elbows, flashes in my mind and I relax even more.

If he wanted to hurt me or take advantage of me, he would have done so last night when I was drunk. He didn't, so he's obviously not that kind of man.

I relax even more and head over to the kitchen. The kitchen counter has the food already laid out and when he sits down on one of the stools, I hesitate for only a moment before I take the one next to him.

"This looks delicious. Thank you."

He grunts, nodding his head as he picks up his own fork.

Guess he isn't much of a talker...

Why does that make me like him so much more? He's cute in a rugged, rough around the edges way. His hair needs a trim, and I never thought that I would go for the big, bulky kind of guy, but something about those tree trunk legs and the way his biceps are testing the strength of his shirt sleeves has my whole body feeling warm.

"I'm Betty, by the way."

"Hayes," he says, his sharp blue eyes flashing over to me and then away again.

I decide not to force small talk. My head is pounding, so I just need to eat and then get the heck out of here.

I bet that my parents are worried sick about me. It was them telling me to stay home and asking if they could hire me another bodyguard that had me going out last night.

I know that they love me and that they just want me to be safe, but I've been kept in the tiny box that they made for me my whole life. I thought that it would get better at college until I saw the bodyguards following me the first day.

They promised that after I graduated, they would stop and so far I haven't seen anyone watching me or wearing the usual bodyguard attire, so I think that they have.

My parents are famous. My dad is an actor that has starred in hundreds of action and romantic comedies, and my mom is a model. The story goes that they went to the same charity event, their eyes locked from across the room, and they've been together ever since.

They had me a few years later, and it's been the three of us ever since. I grew up with security, nannies, and personal chefs. I never wanted for anything, except for maybe a little independence once I was older.

Now that I'm graduating and living on my own, I'm finally getting what I wanted. I moved to the tiny town of Redwood, in the northern part of California. It's close to home, but no one here knows me or cares that my parents are celebrities.

I'm trying to be a screenwriter and I know that I'll occasionally need to go to Los Angeles for business, but the writing part I can do in my tiny one-bedroom apartment.

My place is actually a lot like Hayes's, except I have more color around the place.

"Did you just move in?" I ask and he shakes his head, giving me a side-eyed look.

Okay then.

My eyes go over to the clock on the microwave and my heart jumps into my throat. I'm supposed to meet my parents at my apartment for lunch in half an hour.

"I've got to go. I'm so late," I say, jumping off of the stool.

I wobble in my high heels and Hayes reaches over, grabbing my elbow to steady me. Once I'm good, he grabs our plates and sets them in the sink.

"I'll drive you back to your car," he says and I nod.

I should probably ask him where my car is, but there's no time right now for questions, so I just follow him out of his cute cabin and down the front porch steps to his truck.

Chapter Two

H ayes

I should be used to feeling disappointed by now, but when Betty told me that she didn't remember me or anything that happened last night, I was caught off guard.

I guess I had been hoping that she did. I knew that she had drunk quite a bit, but she still seemed coherent and with it last night when we were at On the Rocks. She was keeping up with our conversation just fine, seemed to be speaking normally, though it was kind of hard to hear her over the music, and was walking fine, but I guess she must have had more than I thought she did.

It was late when we left the bar and so I didn't think that anything was wrong when she fell asleep on the way back to my place.

Looking back now, I can see that I was an idiot to think that she would remember what happened.

I had seen her when she first came in. I was outside on door duty and normally I'm more worried about guys trying to pick a fight to notice any of the girls that come in, but Betty was different. She had my attention from the moment that she walked up to the bar.

I had spent more time at the door, peeking in through the window to keep an eye on her than I did on the actual line trying to get in to see the band that was playing. I felt protective of her instantly, but it was more than that. She called to something inside of me.

Maybe it was because she was the first person to walk through the door who actually smiled at me. I know that people think that I'm scary. I'm six foot seven and I like to work out, so I'm big. The scar that runs down most of the left side of my face doesn't help either.

Being big and mean looking helps make me a great bouncer, but it's not what I really want to do. I love to paint. I used to be a damn good sculptor too, but making art is an expensive hobby and working at On the Rocks pays well, but not that well.

When I had gone inside on my break, it had been easy to pick her out of a crowd. Her red hair was like a flame and I was the moth, incapable of looking away from the light. She had been watching the band, so I didn't try to approach her. I only managed to catch her eye once and, just like at the door, she had smiled at me, her green eyes twinkling.

I kept an eye on her as best I could for the rest of the night and about an hour before closing, I turned around to head back inside from throwing some drunk prick out when I had almost run into her.

She had wobbled in her high heels but she had been doing that all night. It felt natural to reach out and steady her, and I had felt hopeful when she didn't flinch at my touch.

Instead, she had offered to buy me a drink, made me laugh, and then she—

"Where is my car at?" Betty asks, interrupting my memories from last night.

"The bar."

She nods and I wonder where the funny girl from last night is. She probably has a headache and I realize that she should be drinking more water too.

She pushes some of her hair out of her face and I notice how tired she looks.

"You should have slept more."

"What?" she asks, surprised that I broke the silence.

"You look tired. Did I wake you when I was making breakfast?"

I should have been quieter when I first got up or maybe I should have waited until she was awake to start cooking and moving around.

"Oh, no, I didn't hear you at all. I must have really been out," she says with a sigh as she twists her hair over her shoulder. "I always wake up early after I've been drinking. It's like I can't sleep more than four hours or so. As if the hangover isn't punishment enough," she says with a light laugh and I crack a smile.

"Do you go out to drink a lot?"

"No, I was... frustrated last night and decided to go out. Which was a terrible mistake, obviously."

"Why were you frustrated?" I pry.

I want to know everything that I can about this girl. Even if she can't remember what happened last night, I still want her. Maybe I can show her that I'm not a bad guy.

Maybe I can make her fall in love with me too if I can just spend a little more time with her.

"My parents were lecturing me."

"How old are you?" I ask, suddenly alarmed that she's not legal.

"Twenty-one."

"Oh, thank god," I blurt out.

"What?"

"Uh, thank god that you're legal. I didn't want to have let someone underage into the bar last night," I lie and she nods.

"Oh, yeah, you're good."

I am not doing well here. What do people say to get them to like them?

"Why were your parents lecturing you?" I ask, picking back up our conversation.

"This is my first time really away from them. They're both really overprotective of me. Which I know is a good thing. My parents are awesome and I love them so much. I just want to be able to live my own life," she finishes, turning to look out the window.

I want to tell her that she's too precious to be walking around in the world all alone. If she were mine, I would never let her out of my sight. It sounds like that's the opposite of what she wants though, so I'm going to have to get used to it if I want her to be happy with me. Or just get good at trailing her around without being seen.

"I'm sure that they're just worried about you. It will get better soon," I tell her, trying to comfort her.

I don't like when she's upset. It's crazy that I just met this girl and I'm already wrapped around her little finger so tight.

"Do your parents still worry about you?" she asks me, finally turning in her seat to face me again.

"I'm sure that they would, but they're dead."

"Hayes," she starts, her voice filled with pain and concern, but I wave her off.

"It was a while ago."

"When?" she asks quietly and I can feel her eyes on me.

"They died when I was twelve. Car accident."

I rub over the scar on my face and she reaches her hand over the console, her fingers grabbing my forearm and giving me a little squeeze.

"I'm so sorry."

I nod, the ache in my throat starting. It's always the same, every time I think or talk about them and the accident.

She leaves her hand on my arm as we head down Main Street. The roads are quiet, but they almost always are in this small town. I turn into the parking lot of On the Rocks bar and park right next to her car.

I don't want our time to end, but I don't know how to get her to stay. Can I ask her out? Should I invite her back to the bar to see me sometime? See if she wants lunch right now, even though we just had breakfast?

Before I can decide on an approach, she's turning to me with a smile on her face.

"Thank yo—oh crap!" she hisses, and I follow her eyes to where some fancy car is turning into the parking lot.

"What's that?" I ask, my protective instincts on full alert.

"That, is my parents," she says with a sigh as she moves to climb out of my truck.

Chapter Three

B etty

I know that my face is as red as my hair right now because it feels like it's on fire.

I knew that my parents were coming up to visit, see my new apartment, and have lunch with me, so I'm not too surprised to see them pull into the parking lot of On the Rocks. There's always the chance that they were driving by and saw my car so decided to stop, but it's entirely more likely that they have a tracking device on it and that's how they found me.

"Hey guys," I say as I climb out of Hayes's truck.

I try to smooth the wrinkles out of my clothes and tame my hair as I make my way over to them. I'm positive that they think this is a walk of shame and it kind of is, just not in the sex sense.

Their eyes instantly go over my shoulder to where Hayes is climbing out of the driver's side, and I wince.

"This is Hayes. He was just giving me a ride back to my car," I explain, though I don't think that I really just explained anything.

"Hayes, this is my mom and dad, Ryan and Emma Jones."

"Nice to meet you," Hayes says, stepping forward to shake both of their hands.

He steps back after, hovering at my side like he's waiting to rescue me and I have to bite back a smile at his overprotectiveness. He's just as bad as my parents, but I'm finding that I like when he does it more. There's something comforting about having him trailing after me.

"I thought that we were meeting at my place," I say as I turn to face them, and now it's their turn to be embarrassed.

"We saw your car and decided to stop," my mom says, but she's a terrible liar.

I narrow my eyes at her and she winces slightly.

I get my looks from my mom. We have the same red hair and green eyes, the same pale skin and freckles. The only difference is our sizes. Even now, fifteen years after she retired from modeling, she's still a size two. I'm a size sixteen. She towers over me too, almost as tall as my dad. I don't know where I got my height from, but I'm an average five foot six.

"We were worried about you," my dad says, stepping in to bail his wife out.

"Uh-huh," I say and he sighs.

He knows that it's going to be an argument about this later.

I'm surprised that they haven't started lecturing me yet. They told me not to go to a bar last night. They don't want me to go anywhere alone but definitely nowhere alone at night and now here we are, parked outside of one and it's obvious that I didn't go home last night. I think that having Hayes here is stopping them, and I wonder if I could invite him over for lunch without him thinking that I'm a weirdo.

My dad has this stubborn look on his face and I know that as soon as we're alone, he's going to bring up hiring me a bodyguard again. At least now I can prove to them that I went out alone and was totally fine.

A memory from last night hits me. It's of Hayes wrapping a protective arm around my waist while his other hand shoves some guy away from us. I frown, trying to remember what happened before or after, but come up blank.

I look over at Hayes, and he's staring at me. When my eyes meet his, his whole face seems to soften and suddenly he doesn't look so scary anymore.

"Are you hungry?" I ask him, and one corner of his mouth lifts.

"I could eat," he says and I grin.

I know that he's lying, that we both just ate breakfast at his place, but I'm glad that he's willing to step in and save me again.

"We'll meet you back at your apartment," my dad says when I turn back around and I nod.

"I live in Northwoods," I tell Hayes and he nods, knowing where the apartment building is. "Apartment number 202."

I dig my keys out of my purse as I move to get into my car and I see my parents pause. I'm guessing that they want to set a few rules with Hayes, so I just roll my eyes and start my car.

I look over to Hayes before I shift into park, and he gives me a small smile. I smile back as I pull out of my spot.

Getting to my apartment before everyone else isn't a bad idea. I could use a shower and I frown as I wonder just how messy my place is right now. I was in a writing groove, so I haven't picked up in a few days.

I just want it to be nice for when my parents see it for the first time. That's what I tell myself anyway, but as I drive out of the parking lot, it's Hayes that my eyes keep going back to.

Chapter Four

H ayes

"What do you do for a living, Hayes?" Betty's dad, Ryan, asks me as we watch her leave.

"I'm a bouncer here," I tell them, nodding over to the bar behind me.

"Do you like it?" he asks me, and I pause.

No one has ever asked me that.

Do I like it?

Honestly, no. I hate the hours, I hate dealing with a bunch of drunk people all of the time. I hate having to use my looks and height to scare or intimidate people. I hate the guys who see my face or body as a challenge and try to start fights. I just want to stay home and paint, and now that I've found Betty, I just want to take care of her.

"No," I tell him after a beat and he seems pleased by my answer.

"You care about Betty," he says and I shift on my feet.

It almost sounds like a question but he definitely didn't say it like one.

"We could see it in the way that you looked at her," Emma says as she steps into her husband's side.

"Yes."

"We want to offer you a new job then," Ryan says and Emma nods.

"I'm not leaving Redwood," I tell them right away and they smile.

"You won't have to. We want to hire a bodyguard for Betty. She's our baby girl and I know that she wants to spread her wings a bit now that she's graduated, but we worry about her. We're not just around the corner from her anymore and people still recognize her as our daughter, even though she's tried to stay out of the spotlight."

My stomach starts to churn at his words. I had no idea who Betty was last night, but if what her dad says is right, then she could be in danger. I don't like the thought of other people wanting my girl, and I know from last night that she could use someone to look out for her.

That person has to be me. For my sanity at least.

"Okay," I say and Emma grins at me.

"She can't know about this. She won't like it but it will keep her safe and ease our worries," Ryan says and I nod, though uncertainty starts to crawl up my spine.

I don't want Betty to be upset with me, but I need to be close to her. I'm desperate to see her again already and she's only been out of my sights for a few minutes.

"Okay," I say again and they start talking about salary and how often they want me to check in with them.

I let Emma put their phone numbers in my phone and

I'm shaking their hands and climbing into my truck. I follow them across town to Betty's apartment, my head filled with doubts.

I just have to make sure that she never finds out that her parents hired me. When we get married, it won't matter. I just need to get Betty to fall in love with me, and fast.

I stop at a red light and snap out of my thoughts in time to see a police car and ambulance speeding through the intersection.

Just like that, I'm twelve years old and in the back seat of my parents' car. We had been laughing at my mom as she tried to sing along to some song that was on the radio when a truck ran a stop sign and crashed into our car.

I don't remember much from the accident after that. I remember feeling dizzy and wiping the blood from my eyes, but it just kept coming. I couldn't see out of my left eye and I had started to panic and call for my parents, but they never answered me.

Then the firefighters and paramedics were there and getting me out of the back seat. It wasn't until I was in the hospital hours later that a police officer came in to tell me about my parents.

I didn't have any other family, so I went into the system. I hated it. So many of the kids were angry and looking to start a fight, and I was an easy target. I never fought back or defended myself and they got to look like a tough guy who beat up the big, ugly kid. I was always moved after each big fight from one home to the next, and I know that the foster home parents never believed me when I told them that I didn't start it.

The light turns green and I snap out of my memories and hit the gas. I still can't shake the sad feelings though.

After the fourth group home move, I started keeping to myself and became the loner, the outcast, at each place that I went to until I turned eighteen. Then I was on my own.

I bounced around a few different towns before I landed in Redwood, California, and started working at On the Rocks.

I've always had a hard time dealing with all of the emotions of being the sole survivor of the accident. There are times that I wish that I had died too, or that I had died instead of them. In the end though, I had to move on and go on living my life.

Now that I've met Betty, I think I might have finally found out why I was the only one to survive. I was meant to be here so that I can take care of my fiery girl.

I knew that she was meant to be mine when I saw her. She makes me feel alive, she makes me feel seen for the first time since I was twelve years old. It makes me feel like a normal person again and I didn't know how badly I needed that after all of these years.

I pull into Betty's apartment parking lot and park in the first open spot. I can see Ryan and Emma climbing out of their car a few spots over and I roll back my shoulders and climb out of my truck to join them.

I take a deep breath as we head toward the front door and I try to control my heart rate as we head inside and onto the elevator.

It's time for me to start winning my girl over. I need to get my game face on though, because if she finds out about my deal with her parents before I can make her mine, then I don't know what I'll do.

I spend the ride up to her floor trying to calm my racing heart. Betty lives on the fourth floor so I don't have nearly enough time to be prepared to see my girl again.

She smiles at her parents and me as she opens the door and I can see that she's showered and changed her clothes.

"Ready for the tour?" she asks us as she closes the door behind me.

Her parents nod and I have to wonder what they think of her one-bedroom apartment. I admit, I'm a little surprised that she isn't in a fancier place, but I get the feeling that she doesn't want anyone to know who she is, or more accurately, who her parents are.

I can relate to that. I've spent most of my life being that orphaned boy, or the scary boy, or the loser and loner. I liked meeting Betty because she didn't look at me like I was less than her and she didn't act scared of me. She's the first person to treat me like that in a long time.

It's cramped but neat with a small living room that has one love seat, an overstuffed chair in the corner across from the TV stand, and a small desk shoved into the other corner.

The kitchen is just as tiny and I smile when I see that she's stuffed some dirty dishes into the microwave. I stand in front of it so that her parents can't see and when I look over to Betty, she gives me a small smile.

"And then there's the bedroom and bathroom through here," she says and I peek in, taking in the slightly rumpled bed and dresser.

"It looks nice, dear," Emma says, and her husband nods.

I give her a nod too and she smiles, seeming relieved by our reactions to her place.

"Ready for lunch?" Ryan asks and Betty nods, grabbing her shoes and slipping them on as we head back to the front door.

We head around the corner to a local chain restaurant called Woody's. Her parents don't seem off-put as we slide into the booth in the back and I start to relax. I was worried that they would be stuffy or treat me like the help but they both seem really down to earth.

Lunch passes in a blur. I mostly sit there, listening and drinking in everything that I can about my girl. I learn that she loves to read, that she tended to wander off on modeling shoots or film sets. Her favorite food is Italian and that was also her favorite vacation that they took when she was a kid.

Her parents are polite and ask me questions about myself, but there's not much to tell.

"How long have you been in Redwood?" Emma asks as Ryan pays the bill.

"Only about eighteen months," I tell her as I move to pull Betty's chair out for her.

"Do you like it?" she asks, her eyes bouncing between Betty and me.

"I do. I can't stand the traffic in Los Angeles or San Francisco," I admit, and she grins.

"Me either," she whispers conspiratorially.

I give her a small smile and walk with them back out to our cars. Betty rode with her parents, but it seems like they're getting ready to head home.

"I can give you a ride back to your apartment," I offer. "I'm headed that way anyway."

She nods, giving me a smile before she turns back to her parents to hug them goodbye.

"I'll call you later," she promises them and I watch as Emma hugs Betty for a second time, whispering something in her ear that I don't catch.

"It was nice to meet you both," I tell them honestly as I shake both of their hands.

We wave goodbye and I help Betty up into my truck.

"They seemed nice," I say as I start the truck and head back toward her apartment building.

"Thanks. They are," she says as she leans her head against the window.

"Tired?" I ask and she nods, her eyes drooping slightly.

I'm quiet for the rest of the short drive and when we pull into her parking lot, she sits up, yawning as she stretches in her seat.

"Thanks for the ride... and for being a buffer between me and my parents today."

"No problem."

She starts to unbuckle and I know that if I want to ask her out, now is the time to do it.

"We should do it again sometime," I suggest and she frowns. "Not with your parents!"

Man, am I messing this up...

"Like a date?" she asks as she turns to face me more fully and I nod.

"Yeah, a date."

"Okay," she says with a shy smile.

Her cheeks turn a pale shade of pink and my stomach flips.

"Tomorrow?" I ask, and she nods, biting down on the full bottom lip.

"Here, I'll give you my number."

I pass her my phone and watch as she adds her phone number and calls herself.

"I'll call you," I promise her, and she gathers her things and moves to get out of the truck.

I jump out too, rounding the hood and helping her down.

"See you tomorrow," she says, her hand squeezing mine as she passes me and heads for the front door.

I watch her go, my heart in my throat, and I know then that I need Betty in my life.

I can not mess this up.

Chapter Five

B etty

"This is really nice," I tell Hayes as we take our seats at the cute little bistro in town.

He smiles at me across the table, looking relieved as he picks up his menu.

"I wasn't sure what you were hungry for, but this is the top listing when you search for best date places in Redwood," he tells me and I grin.

He seems so nervous and he's still so thoughtful and earnest when he talks to me. He's adorable, which is a word that I'm not sure anyone has used to describe Hayes before.

"Well, I love it. I've never been here before. Or on a date," I admit, deciding to put all of my cards out there on the table.

"Me either," he says, a faint pink flush staining his cheekbones.

We share a smile before we both start to look over the menu. I thought that I would be nervous to go on my first date, but being with Hayes is easy. It feels natural to sit across from him and none of the date jitters that I thought that I would experience have come.

"What looks good?" Hayes asks once I set my menu aside and I open my mouth to tell him when the waiter heads to our table and interrupts me.

"Welcome to Amelia's Bistro. Can I get you started with something to drink?" she asks and I can't help but notice the way that her eyes keep straying to Hayes.

"Can I get a water, please?"

"Me too," Hayes says, and she nods as she scribbles it down on her pad.

"Are you ready to order now too?" she asks, her eyes landing on Hayes once again and possessiveness starts to flood my body.

Can she not see me? Does she not realize that this is a date?

"I think so. Are you ready, boo?" I ask Hayes and he raises his eyebrow at my term of endearment.

"Yeah, you go first... baby," he says, trying out one of his own pet names.

I grin as I grab my menu and rattle off my order.

"I'll have the bistro burger with the sweet potato fries."

"I'll have the same," Hayes says and she nods, shooting him a smile but he's too busy looking over at me to notice her.

"I'll get that right out for you," she tries again and I can see when she finally gets the clue and gives up on flirting with him.

We both ignore her, and I smile to myself as she turns and leaves.

"I think that she likes you."

"I doubt it," Hayes says and he sounds so sure of himself that it kind of breaks my heart.

He's so positive that no one could ever like him or find him attractive that it makes me want to show him how amazing he is. I know that I barely know him, but I can tell that he's a good one.

"So, tell me about yourself," I say after the waitress drops off our waters.

"What do you want to know?"

"Where are you from?"

"Sequoia. You probably haven't heard of it but it's a small town in Southern California."

"Yeah! It's like an hour, hour and a half from Los Angeles, right?"

"Yeah, it's more of a college town. My dad was a professor at the university there and my mom ran a coffee shop right off of campus."

"Did you like it?"

"Yeah, I like the small town more and it would get pretty empty during the summer, so there weren't any lines at the movie theater or skate park."

"Best of both worlds then."

"Exactly. What about you? Did you like living in Los Angeles?"

"Not really. Too many people, too much traffic, and users."

"You like the small-town life then, huh?" he asks and I nod.

"I'd rather take it slow than live in a big city like Los Angeles."

"Me too," he admits.

"Here're your burgers," the waitress says, and I blink, looking away from Hayes's magnetic gaze.

"This looks delicious," I say as I grab my burger and take a bite.

I moan and Hayes freezes with his own burger halfway to his mouth. I drag the back of my hand across my mouth, wondering if I have some ketchup or something on my face. Hayes clears his throat and takes a big bite of his burger before I can ask him if there's something on my face and so I shrug and go back to eating. The food is delicious and we both clean our plates quickly.

"What made you move to Redwood?" I ask between bites of my crème brûlée dessert.

"I was kind of bouncing around, trying to find a place that felt like home, and then I got a job at On the Rocks and found my cabin," he says with a shrug.

"And does it feel like home?" I ask and he looks up at me.

"It didn't before, but lately it's started to," he says quietly and I can feel my face heating.

The check comes and Hayes pays it, waving off my offer to split it with him. It isn't until we were in his truck and headed back to my place that I realize he never once asked me a question about my parents or any of the celebrities that I've met.

I can't remember the last time that that's happened. Usually everyone is clamoring to get some gossip or to be my friend in the hopes that my family's connections can help them out in their own career.

It's been nice to not have to worry about that with Hayes.

"Can I walk you up?" he asks almost shyly and I nod.

"Yeah, I'd like that."

He hops out of the truck and jogs around to my side, offering me his hand as he helps me out. Neither one of us lets go as he closes the door and we start to walk toward my building.

"I had a lot of fun tonight," I tell him as he hits the button for the elevator and he smiles.

"Me too. We should do it again sometime," he says and I can see him looking at me out of the corner of his eye.

"Yeah, we should," I say as the elevator doors open and he looks so happy to hear me say yes to another date with him that my heart starts to beat in double time in my chest.

As soon as the elevator doors open, I know that something is wrong. There's too much noise for my tiny little apartment building and as we step off, my body goes stiff.

I can feel Hayes tense beside me, his hand tightening around mine as we watch the police officers milling around my hallway.

"What happened?" I ask one of my neighbors.

She's an elderly lady that I've seen around but haven't gotten the chance to introduce myself to yet.

"Break in. They got away with a bunch of stuff, I hear. Mr. Andrews came home and surprised them, and now he's being taken to the hospital."

My stomach knots and I feel like I might throw up my dinner.

"Pack your stuff," Hayes tells me as he takes in the scene and I frown up at him.

"What?" I ask him and he looks down, meeting my eyes.

"You need to pack your stuff. You can't stay here."

I suppose he has a point. I don't know that I could sleep when I know that someone had broken in right next door earlier that day.

"Right," I say and he leads me over to my apartment,

waiting while I get my keys out of my purse and unlock the door.

"Just get the essentials tonight. We can come back for everything else tomorrow."

I frown at his choice of words but don't argue with him. My head is still on the robbery and poor Mr. Andrews.

I don't have a lot of stuff unpacked yet so that makes grabbing a suitcase easier. Hayes is looking over all of the boxes that are stacked up against my living room wall but he turns when he hears me come in, his eyes scanning my face in concern.

"I'm alright. It just caught me off guard."

He nods, taking the suitcase from me and grabbing my hand with his free one. He lets me go long enough for me to lock the door behind me and then we're headed back out to his truck.

We don't talk as we drive back to his cabin. I'm too busy wondering if I should call my parents and let them know or not. I'm sure that they'll find out about it at some point, but I don't want to deal with that headache right now.

I sigh as Hayes pulls into his driveway and he helps me out of the truck before he grabs my suitcase and leads me inside.

"I'll take the couch," he says right away and I smile.

"I don't want to put you out, Hayes. I'm sure that the bed is big enough."

"It's okay. Make yourself at home," he says with a smile as he sets my suitcase down on top of the dresser. "I'm going to take a quick shower before bed."

I nod, watching him as he looks around the bedroom. He's so cute and a part of me wants to walk over to him and kiss him right now, but it just doesn't seem like the right time, so I bite my bottom lip and watch him walk out of the bedroom.

I'm determined to tell him that we can share the bed once he gets out of the shower, but as I change into my pajamas and lie down, I can't seem to keep my eyes open.

I'll just close them for a moment, I think and just like that, I'm out.

Chapter Six

H ayes

I want to paint her so badly.

Betty is all color. Her bright red hair, those green eyes, her sunny smile. Looking at her has my fingers itching for a paintbrush so that I can try to capture her essence on canvas.

"I'll do the dishes since you cooked breakfast," she says with a smile as she pops the last bite of her toast into her mouth.

Her little pink tongue darts out, licking off any stray crumbs and I shift in my stool, trying to make room in my jeans for my growing cock.

Being around Betty is a sweet kind of torture.

"Are you working today?" she asks me and I shake my head.

"No, I'm off again today and then on for the next four nights."

"Cool, then we can hang out together. Maybe we could watch a movie or something," she says as she hops down from the stool and carries her dishes over to the sink.

"Sure, whatever you want."

She hums as she looks under the sink for something and I frown.

"What are you doing?" I ask as I move to join her.

"I was looking for the dish soap."

"It's right here."

She smiles as I pass her the bottle of Dawn.

"It's going to sound weird, but I love doing the dishes."

"Really?"

"Oh, yeah," she says with a self-conscious laugh. "I think it was because we always had help around growing up, so I never really got to do it for myself. Then when I first went to college, I ate at the cafeteria, so I still didn't have to do them."

"When did you move out of the dorms?" I ask her as I grab a dish towel and start drying.

"The first chance that I got. It was my sophomore year since we were required to live on campus for our first one."

I nod and she goes on.

"My parents got me this really fancy place close to campus, which was cool. I didn't really like living with a bunch of roommates, so it worked out in that way."

"I don't like living with roommates either," I admit and she smiles at me as she passes me a plate.

"You like your space."

I nod even though it wasn't a question.

"Me too. Anyway, I was on my own for the first time and I

got to do all of the cleaning and cooking. It was a struggle at first but then I started to enjoy it. I was responsible for me. I got to make all of the decisions and build something by myself."

"You were independent."

"Yeah, for the first time in nineteen years, and it was awesome. I mean, I know that my parents still had body-guards and security on me and they insisted on having cleaners come in once a month to do a deep clean, but I like to think that there wasn't much for them to do because I was already so tidy."

She smiles, clearly proud of the memory, and I fall a little more in love with her.

"Your parents seemed nice," I start and she smiles.

"They are. For celebrities, they're still pretty down to earth. They just worry too much about me. If it were up to them, I would still be living with them. They like to wrap me in bubble wrap, but I want to get out more."

"I'm sure most parents worry like that."

"I know, I know, and when I have kids of my own, I'll probably be just like them. It's just frustrating for me now."

The thought of her pregnant with our kids has my cock hardening even more in my jeans.

"Do you want kids?"

"Sure! Well... in a few years," she says with a grin as she passes me a glass.

I can work with that.

"So, you never wanted to be a star like your parents?" I ask curiously and she snorts.

"God no. Fame is crazy. I don't want my every move to be scrutinized. I don't want to live in the public eye at all. Plus, I don't have the height or body to be a model or—"

"Yes, you do," I interrupt her and she blushes.

"And I never liked acting. I'd much rather work behind the scenes or on the other side of the camera."

"Be a director?" I ask, and she shakes her head.

"Screenwriter."

"Ah, that explains why you brought your computer with you last night."

She grins at that, passing me the last glass before she pulls the plug and lets the sink drain.

"I love writing. I took this creative writing course my freshman year and just fell in love with it."

"Well, I look forward to watching one of your movies soon then."

She beams at that and it has my own lips tugging up.

"Want to have a movie day?" she asks me and I'm powerless to say anything but yes.

She races to the living room as soon as the word is out of my mouth and I follow her, veering into the bedroom to grab us some blankets and pillows.

She pulls up Netflix as I get settled on the couch and it's then I learn just how much Betty loves movies. She talks throughout them, explaining plot points or what she would do differently. She keeps apologizing for interrupting, staying quiet for a few minutes, and then doing it again. If anyone else did it, I would find it annoying, but when Betty does it, it's just adorable.

If I didn't think that I was in love with her before, that would have tipped me off.

We make popcorn after the first movie is over and Betty tells me about some of the times that she went to set with her dad when she was growing up. She never talks much about the actors. Instead, she's focused on how the director acted, the way that they looked at a script, or the decisions that the costume department made.

It's obvious that she loves it and I'm happy to sit beside her and soak up every word that comes out of her beautiful mouth.

After the second movie, when we're in the kitchen making sandwiches, she turns to me with a smile.

"I meant to ask you. Did you go to college?"

"No, I didn't have the money," I admit and her smile fades.

"Do you like being a bouncer?"

"No."

"What do you want to do instead?" she asks as she finishes her sandwich and pours some chips onto her plate.

"I love to paint."

"Are you any good?" she asks curiously and I smile.

"Yes."

"Can I see any of your work?"

I nod to the wall behind the couch where there's a giant canvas of a mountain lake. The mountains and trees are reflected back in the water with just a hint of the sun setting in the corner.

"You did that?" Betty half shouts as she abandons her food and rushes over to the painting.

"Yeah. It was a few years ago. I haven't painted much in the last few months."

"You should! You're really good," she says, her eyes dancing over the canvas as she takes everything in.

"Thanks."

I carry both of our plates over to the living room and when Betty still continues to stare at the painting, I go back and grab us each a glass of water.

"You should quit being a bouncer and sell your art," she says as we take our seats once more.

I smile softly and shake my head.

"I wish, but it's hard to break into the art world," I say and she nods.

"Maybe my parents know someone that could help," she starts, and I shake my head.

"I don't want to do it that way," I tell her and she stares at me with a funny look on her face for a minute before she leans over and kisses me.

She catches me off guard and I almost drop my sandwich on the floor as I move to kiss her back.

We fumble together for a minute, trying to get our heads angled right and our hands around each other.

I've never kissed a woman before, but even in my wildest dreams, it was never as good as kissing Betty is. She's warm and pliant beneath me, her lips molding perfectly to mine.

When her little tongue darts out and swipes against my bottom lip, I have to grit my teeth to stop from coming in my jeans.

My hands smooth up and down her back, inching lower with each pass, and I wish that she was straddling me so that I could feel her on me, my hands cupping her lush ass as she rocked against me. I wish that we weren't wearing so many layers. I want to feel her hands on me, on my bare skin.

She inches closer to me, her hands stroking across my chest and up to my shoulders. I wonder if she can feel my heartbeat racing out of control beneath her fingers. I wonder if her heart is beating even close to as fast as mine.

She breaks away from me with a gasp, her chest rising and falling fast as we both suck in lungfuls of air. The movie is long forgotten in the background and she tilts her chin up, her gaze snagging on my lips, and I can't help but groan at the hungry look in her eyes.

"Betty," I say roughly, my voice holding a plea.

I don't know what else to say. I want to beg her to never stop kissing me. I want to do so much more than just kiss her.

"I don't want you to stop," Betty admits, her voice no more than a whisper, but I hear it.

Her lips land back on mine, her arms circling my neck as I grab her hips and drag her onto my lap. She wraps herself tighter around me, her knees digging into the couch on either side of me as I lean back against the cushions.

Betty moans as she finds the hard ridge in my jeans and I break away from her lips when she squirms on top of me. I bite back a curse as her eyes fall closed, her red hair cascading down her back as she tilts her face up to the ceiling and moans.

"Mine," I murmur and she looks down, her eyes half mast as they meet mine.

"Hmm?" she asks, her fingers digging into my shoulders as she rocks on top of me.

"You're beautiful," I tell her instead.

I have a feeling that she's not ready to hear that she's mine just yet.

Betty smiles down at me, her head tipping toward mine and her hair falls around us in a curtain as we go back to making out. Her lips angle against mine, claiming me, marking me, just as I claim her. I moan, letting her have access to all of me.

Pleasure slides into my belly, sticky and hot as Betty grinds on top of me. My hands move over her, trying to touch her everywhere. On her ass, in her hair, molding her curves.

I get lost in her, in the feel of her lips against mine, our tongues tangling together. It's like we can't get close enough to each other, like we're both trying to absorb each other, to make us one.

I rock my hips up against hers, needing more pressure, and Betty moans against my mouth, obviously loving the added dynamic. Her fingers dig into my shoulders, hard enough to leave bruises, but I don't care. I want to be marked by her. I want to look in the mirror and see every place that she's touched me.

Betty rips her mouth away from mine once again, her lips swollen from mine, her cheeks a rosy red, and her eyes filled with lust. I know that I could have her right now, but I don't want to rush things between us.

I'm saved from saying anything though when her phone rings. She groans as she rolls off of me and plops back down on the couch.

We're both still breathing hard as she grabs her phone and gives me an apologetic smile as she moves toward the bedroom to answer the call.

I watch her go and then lean forward to grab the remote and pause the movie.

I take the next five minutes while she's on the phone to get myself under control. When she joins me once again on the couch, I'm almost there.

Then she smiles at me, her green eyes shining and I'm back to square one.

When she falls asleep after the next movie, I scoop her up in my arms and carry her to bed. As I tuck her in, I wonder if tomorrow night I'll be sleeping beside her in it.

Chapter Seven

Betty

How did I end up living with Hayes?

That's a good question. I meant to go back home, I swear, but his place is so cozy. He keeps bringing me food, so I just stay. Maybe I should ask him about when he wants me to leave, but I don't think that he does. Besides, it's not like I was really in any rush to head back to my place. It feels depressing after being in Hayes's space the last few days.

We've settled into a new routine since that first night. He makes us breakfast and I help clean up. Then we either run errands or curl up on the couch to talk and watch movies. When he goes to work, I grab my laptop and write until he comes home. Some nights I don't manage to stay awake until he's back, but I always wake up tucked into his bed in the morning, my laptop charging on the dresser.

Hayes is way too good to me. He's unlike anyone that I've ever met before. When he had turned down my offer of having my parents help him make connections in the art world, I knew that he was the one for me. He's not using me to get to my parents or for help with his career. He just likes me for me.

We haven't gone past making out and dry humping on his couch, but I'm ready to. I've been trying to tempt him by wearing some of my old clothes that fit me a little tighter and I can tell that he likes it, but he hasn't made a move.

I'm hoping that changes soon though. I love his bedroom, but I want to finally share that big bed with him.

"Hey," Hayes says as he pokes his head around the bedroom door.

He's grinning and I can't help but match his energy. I sit up in bed, wondering what's gotten into him and he opens the door wider and steps inside.

"I'm glad that you're up. I have a surprise for you," he says as he comes over to help me out of bed.

He takes my hand and I try to think of what he could have gotten me. He leads me out into the living room and I step out from behind him, my eyes instantly landing on the new desk on the far wall.

There's a desktop monitor set up on top of it and my laptop is already plugged in and resting on a stand. There's a new desk chair tucked under the desk.

"I thought you should have a place to work besides the couch," Hayes tells me as he tugs me over closer to the new furniture.

I lean into his side as my eye start to water.

"You did all of this for me?" I ask him, turning in his arms to look up at him.

"I want you to be happy here," he says quietly, pushing some of my hair out of my face so he can see more clearly.

"I am," I tell him, and I mean it.

I love Hayes. He treats me like a queen and seems to live to make me happy. How could you not fall in love with someone who treats you like that?

I open my mouth, wanting to tell him how I feel, but Hayes leans down, his lips capturing mine before I can get the words out.

Then I'm lost in him.

It was like this when we kissed last night too. He becomes my whole world as soon as his lips are on mine. If my parents hadn't called me, I wonder just how far things would have gone.

Part of me wishes that they hadn't interrupted us. I had been so worked up that sitting next to him for the rest of the movie was unbearable.

His tongue licks the seam of my lips and I open for him eagerly, letting him tangle our tongues together as I cling to him. I want to climb him. I want to rub myself against him just like last night and he must want that too because he cups my ass and lifts me.

I wrap myself around him, moaning into his mouth as his big, meaty paws mold me to him.

"We don't have to do anything that—"

"I want to," I tell him breathlessly and he lets out a groan.

"Thank god," he mutters, and then we're moving.

He carries me into the bedroom and I expect him to drop me onto the bed, but he holds me. It's like he doesn't want to let me go just yet and that's fine with me because I don't want to be anywhere but in his arms.

"I'm a virgin," I manage to tell him between kisses and he moans, kissing me back harder.

"So am I."

There's a part of my brain that is shocked by that and I have a million questions but I don't ask any of them. I don't want to break the bubble that we're in or ruin the moment.

My fingers trace over the scar on his forehead as I thread my fingers through his hair and he shivers. I want to tell him that I don't mind the scar but I can't seem to take my mouth off of his long enough to do that.

He moves us closer to the bed and lays me down gently on the mattress. I'm still in my pajamas and he leans up as his fingers slip into the waistband, meeting my eyes as he slowly peels them down my legs.

I lift my hips when he comes back for my panties, wanting to help him get them off as fast as possible.

It feels like I'm burning up as he slowly undresses me, but the torture of waiting to see what he'll do next is adding to my desire.

He leans over me, giving me a sweet kiss before he moves lower, kissing me between my breasts over my pajama top. Then he's pulling that up and over my head.

I've never been naked in front of anyone before and the self-conscious part of me instinctively starts to move to cover my stomach and other problem areas, but Hayes stops me.

"Let me look," he growls, and I rest my hands back down on the mattress.

His eyes heat as he takes me in, and I squirm under his gaze.

"I need," I start as I lean up on my elbows but he interrupts me.

"I know what you want, want you need. I was put on this earth to give it to you."

I think that my ovaries just exploded.

I fall back, bouncing on the mattress slightly, my breasts and stomach jiggling as he settles between my legs.

He grips my knees, forcing my legs open wider and I bite my bottom lip as his head moves closer. His breath fans over my slick folds and I bite my lip harder, trying to hold in my moan but it's no use.

As soon as his tongue licks up my center, my mind blanks and all I become is feeling.

His slow movements are driving me out of my mind and I lift my hips, desperate for him to go faster, harder, something.

"More," I whine and I swear that he grins against my pussy.

He sucks my clit into his mouth and I suck in a sharp breath as my first orgasm slams into me. From there, it's all a blur.

I call out his name, my heels digging into his shoulders and my fingers tangling in his hair as he licks me completely and thoroughly, to one orgasm and then another. I'm hoarse and shaking as Hayes gives me one last lick and looks up my body to my face.

I try to move my head, wanting to memorize the sight of him between my thighs, but I'm wrung out. My entire body feels weightless and I try to cling on to Hayes so that I don't float up to the ceiling.

He starts to kiss his way up my body as I lie there trying to catch my breath. His journey takes him over my rounded stomach and higher, until he's reached my breasts. His big hands squeeze them gently, plumping them up as he leans over me and starts to lap at the stiff peaks.

"Hayes!" I groan, not sure that I can take any more orgasms.

He just smiles though and switches over to my other breast. My eyes fall closed as pleasure rolls through me and I stop trying to fight him on giving me pleasure.

He squeezes the soft mounds slightly, holding them in place as he licks and sucks my nipples. With each lick and suck and flick, an answering reaction goes off between my legs. By the time Hayes releases my breasts, I'm a writhing, panting mess and wanting more than just his mouth between my legs.

"Hayes, I need you," I plead and he nods, the hunger in his eyes visible, even in the dim lighting.

He kisses me once more, slowly, before he stands by the side of the bed and strips off his clothes. I wonder if I should offer to suck his cock, but before I can decide, he's back and kneeling between my legs. I watch as he fists his cock, stroking it once, twice, teasing me and turning me on all at once.

"Hayes," I plead.

He meets my eyes, leaning forward and guiding the tip of his dick to my slick opening. My back arches as he starts to push in and he hisses. I know that he's reached my virginity and I look up at him, showing him how much I trust him, how much I want him.

"I don't want to hurt you," he says and I can tell the words are killing him. The thought of hurting me is obviously abhorrent to him.

"You won't. You've already made me feel so good," I tell him softly and he nods.

He thrusts into me fully and I suck in a breath. The sting of pain isn't as bad as I thought it would be, probably from all of the orgasms that he's already given me, and it's over in a few seconds, leaving only a feeling of fullness behind.

I rock my hips against his, trying to test out the feeling more and Hayes bites out a curse, burying his face in my neck.

"Easy, Betty," he breathes, but I can't stop.

Eventually, Hayes raises his face and starts to move with me. His pace is slow at first, letting me get used to him moving inside of me. Every part of me tingles and I close my eyes, trying to embrace the feelings fully.

I wrap my legs around his waist, gasping and then moaning as he hits a special spot deep inside of me.

"That's it," Hayes says encouragingly as he grabs one of my thighs and holds me in place as his pace picks up more and he starts to pound into me.

My orgasm comes out of nowhere, hitting me hard and fast. I moan as it slams into me like a crescendo, echoing throughout, like a wave starting deep in my core and lapping out to my entire body.

"Hayes, Hayes, Hayes," I chant as my fingernails dig into his shoulders.

"Betty," he moans and I feel his warmth spread inside of me.

He holds himself above me and our gazes clash, staying on each other as we both come down from our collective high, and I swear I can see love shining in his eyes.

I wonder if he can see it in mine too.

Chapter Eight

H ayes

I was trying not to wake Betty as I got ready for work. We've been fucking like rabbits since this morning and I know that she must be exhausted. I was planning on heading to work and then coming home and slipping into bed with her, but as the shower door opens and she steps in, I get the feeling that that's not going to happen.

I turn, capturing her waist in my hands and pressing her against me so that she can be under the water too.

"What are you doing up?" I ask her as I nuzzle her neck.

"Thought you might like some company," she says, her eyes full of mischief.

When her hand slips between us and wraps around my rapidly hardening cock, I know what she's really after.

I step back, giving her more room to work and admiring the view as I go.

She's the most beautiful woman that I've ever seen. Her bare legs are pale in the light and look like fresh cream. There's water dripping off of her hair, rolling down her shoulders to the peaks of her breasts and my mouth waters, dying to lick up those drops.

Betty wiggles against me, and I reach out, cupping her face in my hands.

"I knew when I first saw you that I was never going to be able to let you go," I breathe as I lower my mouth to hers.

Betty moans out my name in that breathy way of hers that drives me crazy, her nails scratching along my scalp as her fingers twist in my hair. Her tongue slides against mine, twisting around mine as we make out like teenagers.

It's obvious by the way that she's moving against me though that she wants more, so I reach down, grabbing her ass and lifting her against me.

She shivers as I press her against the cold shower tile but never stops kissing me. When her hips rock against me, trying to get my cock to slip into her snug opening, I oblige her.

Her legs circle around my waist, wrapping tight as she moves against me, and I nip her bottom lip, feeling her need surging with each stroke.

Her back arches, pushing her tits up into my face and I can't resist that offer. I duck my head, wrapping my lips around one of her nipples and suckling the hard point.

Her fingers tighten in my hair and she cries out, her hips moving against me faster. She urges me on, and just like earlier, I lose control, pounding into her like a beast.

I can tell from the noises she's making and by the way she's tugging on my hair that she's close. Her heels dig into my ass, urging me to go faster, harder, to give her more.

I moan, my eyes finding hers as we both go flying over the edge.

"Is it like this for everyone?" she breathes out and I shake my head.

"I don't know," I admit and she leans forward, kissing me.

I want to tell her that I love her, but I bite the words back.

It's only been a few days and I don't want to scare her off. I can't scare her off.

I need her.

We laugh as I try to wash her off and hold her up at the same time. When she almost slips, I reluctantly let her go.

She grabs the soap from me and washes my back as I shampoo my hair. This is something that I never thought that I would have. No one ever looked twice at me, unless it was in fear.

No one until my Betty.

"I'm going to be late for work," I groan when we come out of the bathroom and I finally catch sight of the alarm clock.

"Sorry," Betty says with a giggle as she walks past me and wraps her arms around my waist.

Her chin rests on my chest as she looks up at me, a breathtaking glow covering her features.

I grin down at her.

"Liar," I tease and she smirks at me.

"It was worth it," she says as she steps away from me.

I try to grab her but she's already rounding to the other side of the bed, so I head to the closet and decide to get ready for work.

Betty is right though. It was worth it.

I watch her as she heads over to the dresser and pulls out a pair of jeans and a tank top.

"Where are you going?" I ask as I pull on my own jeans and grab one of the plain black shirts with *Bouncer* on the back out of my closet.

"To work with you. I'm ahead on writing so I can take the night off and spend it with you. It would probably be better if I got some fresh air anyway," she says as she grabs her shoes.

I want to tell her to stay here. The last thing that I need is to worry about some guys hitting on her all night, but she looks so happy to be going with me that I can't find it in me to tell her no.

"All set?" I ask her as she grabs her purse and she nods and takes my hand as we head out.

It's a short ride to On the Rocks and I lead her inside, finding her a place at the bar where I know that the bartenders will be able to keep an eye on her.

Theo, my boss, is behind the counter when we walk in and he nods at Betty and me before I head into the back to put my stuff in my locker. I'm about to close it when I get a call from Ryan.

I've been trying to ignore him and Emma for the last few days. I'm still making sure that she's safe, but I doubt that they would appreciate me sleeping with their daughter when I'm supposed to be keeping her out of trouble. I hit ignore, promising myself that I'll call him back tomorrow. I send him a text, telling him that I'm at work and will call him later before I shove my phone into my pocket and head back out to Betty.

Theo is now in his office as I pass, riffling through all of the papers on his desk. The coffee pot is brewing and I know that he must have just put on a fresh pot. The guy downs coffee all night long, so I'm not sure how he manages to sleep.

An ugly orange futon is in the corner of his office, but I doubt that he's ever slept on that thing. Although if he doesn't, then I don't know why he keeps the thing. It's a real eyesore.

"Hey, Hayes," Theo says as he looks up from his desk.

"Hey, how's it going?" I ask as I lean against his office door.

"Good," he says as he looks through a few more papers.

"How's Emmaline?" I ask and he instantly smiles.

He finally admitted that he was in love with his best friend's little sister a few weeks ago and got together with her.

"Good. She just started college, so she's excited about her new classes."

"What's she majoring in again?"

"Business," he says and it's cute how proud he is of her.

"I better get to work," I say and he nods, going back to his papers.

The bar is about to open, and I nod to Haven and Briony as I pass them on my way to Betty. They're used to me keeping to myself, so my usual nod isn't out of the ordinary but I can see both of them giving Betty curious looks.

"Want to sit outside with me?" I ask her and she nods, so I grab a stool in one hand and her hand in my other and we push out into the night.

It's still early as I get her set up off to the side of the front door and she leans her head back, looking up at the stars that are just starting to peek out.

"Have you ever been camping?" she asks and I nod.

"Yeah, my parents and I used to go when I was younger.

I haven't been in a while," I say as I look up at the darkening night sky.

"Would you take me sometime?" she asks quietly, and I nod.

"Sure. Where do you want to go?"

That's all I need to say and she's launching into all of the places that she wants to see. She's been to all of the major cities growing up, so now she wants to see Yellowstone, Mackinac Island, and some tiny town in Italy that I've never even heard of.

I promise myself that I'll find a way to take her to all of those places.

She's pulling up pictures on her phone when the first customers start to trickle in. The music kicks up even louder and Betty shifts closer to me so we don't have to scream to be heard over it.

"See? It's called Termoli." She shows me the map and then switches over to images.

I can't deny that it looks like a pretty place, but it's Betty's excitement that has the corners of my lips kicking up.

I wave some more people in, taking the stool next to her as she starts to look up camping gear.

"I have a sleeping bag," I tell her when she pulls up that page and she grins at me.

"Would we just need one?" she asks with a wink and I laugh.

"I'm not sure that we'd both fit, but we can try."

She grins at me and then goes back to looking at her phone. A pang of guilt hits me when I think about the last message that I got on my own phone and I wonder if I should just tell her right now that her parents technically hired me to be her bodyguard.

I know that she'll react badly though, and I don't want her to be stranded here with me. I have a feeling that she'll try to walk home and it's already dark out, so I can't have that.

I mean, I haven't gotten paid yet and there's still time for me to quit and refuse payment, so maybe she never has to know.

I know that that's what I'll be telling her parents tomorrow when I call them, but I can't seem to shake the weird feeling in my gut that tells me this is still going to backfire on me. Even as Betty starts to debate the merits of a tent versus an RV, it's still there and when we head home after my shift, I hold her a little tighter, wondering if this will be the last time that she's in my arms.

Chapter Nine

B etty

I smile as I leave the store but that smile quickly fades when I see how hard it's raining.

I'm out running some errands while Hayes does his laundry and some other chores around the house. I was supposed to run to the grocery store, office store, and then pop over to the arts and crafts store, but now I'm debating if I should avoid the bad weather and roads and just head home.

So far, I've only gone to the arts and craft store and I bite my lip, weighing my options. I really only went out today because I wanted to do something nice for Hayes. He's been so generous with me. I smile every time I sit down at my new desk and I wanted to try to repay him in some way.

The only problem is, what do you get the guy who

doesn't seem to want anything but you? When the idea hit me this morning, I knew that I needed to go out right away and get it.

"I can go grocery shopping and run errands tomorrow," I tell myself, clutching the canvases and other supplies that I bought to surprise Hayes tighter as I start to run across the parking lot to my car.

I turn the heat on as soon as I start the car, aiming it at my hair in an attempt to dry it off a little bit. When I flip down the mirror, I sigh. I'm a mess. Water is dripping onto my shoulders and I'm drenched even though I had a parking spot close to the front door.

My red hair is hanging limp around me and plastered to my face in other places. Raindrops drip off of my nose and lips and I lick them away, trying to dry my face off on my shirt but it's just as wet as the rest of me.

I pull out of the lot and turn toward home.

Home.

When did I start thinking of Hayes's place as my home?

I mull that over, wondering if I should be freaked out at how fast our relationship has gone, but I'm oddly calm about it.

Hayes is amazing. He's so sweet and attentive. He has been since the first night that we met, even though I don't really remember meeting him.

He must feel the same way too because he hasn't asked me to leave yet and it's been over a week now. I wonder if he can feel the connection between us like I can.

My mind flashes back to that first morning that I woke up in his bed. He wanted to say something then. I remember the look he had when he realized that I didn't remember anything from the night before.

I had put it out of my mind, but now I'm dying to know

why he was so upset and what happened between us that night.

I'll just ask him in a minute, I think as I pull into his driveway.

I grab the canvases and painting supplies that I bought for him and make a mad dash for the front door.

It's still pouring outside and maybe that's why Hayes doesn't hear me come inside. I can hear him talking to someone, so I try to be quiet so that I don't disturb him. Another part of me wants to eavesdrop. I haven't seen or heard him talking to anyone really since I got here and I'm curious about any friends that he might have.

"Yeah... I know, I'm sorry about that. I was at work... okay."

His side of the conversation isn't giving much away and I smile. Hayes is a man of few words so I guess I shouldn't be surprised that he seems to talk even less when he's on the phone.

I bend over, intending on setting the gifts down by the front door so that I can get out of my wet clothes. Maybe I can convince Hayes to join me in the shower and help warm me up.

I grin to myself, imagining him turning around and seeing me naked.

He'd be on me before I could make it to the bedroom, I think with a soft giggle.

I want that though. I always want him around me. Maybe it's time that I finally pulled my big girl panties up and told him how I feel about him. I'm sure that he must be feeling it too, right? So, if I tell him that I love him, he can say it back and then we can do my shower idea.

I have my plan all set until Hayes opens his mouth and says what he says next.

"I know, Mr. Ambrose. You don't need to worry. She's safe. Yes, I've been keeping an eye on her. After the break-in, I moved her in with me."

My stomach drops at his words.

He's talking to my dad? And what does he mean that he's been keeping an eye on me? Oh my god. They hired him to be my bodyguard. But when? Was he meant to protect me at the bar the night that we met? Or did they hire him later, when they met in the parking lot? Did he ask me out so that he could make sure I was safe? Am I here so that he could do his job easier?

A million thoughts race through my head, none of them good, and I don't know what I should do now. Get out of here before he can see me and know that I overheard? Maybe I can get a ticket somewhere else and block all of them.

My eyes flick over to the desk where my laptop is and I wonder if it would be worth it to leave without that and all of the work that I have saved on it. I bite my lip, debating for a moment before I realize that yes, it would be. I need to get out of here now before I break down in front of him or tip off my parents to how mad I am at them.

I'm not sure who I'm more upset with. My parents for breaking a promise, or Hayes for leading me on and breaking my heart.

It's Hayes. It's definitely Hayes.

My stomach roils and I think I might throw up. I go to clutch my stomach and the art stuff falls from my numb fingers, hitting the ground with a bang.

Hayes spins around, his eyes wide as he sees me standing there and I can tell the moment that he realizes that I heard him.

I'm not sure when I started to cry but now the tears are

coming fast, spilling down my cheeks faster than the rain is coming down outside.

I straighten my shoulders, intending on walking out of here with my head held high but I can't seem to be able to get my feet to move.

I can feel the heat spreading on my face, making it as red as my hair. My throat and eyes feel gritty and I'm not even doing that good a job of holding back the tears.

"You're my bodyguard?" I whisper, forcing the words out of my tight throat.

"Betty, I can explain," Hayes starts, his hands held out in front of him like he's approaching a wild animal.

I don't wait for his explanation. It's not worth it. Not when I can see the truth all over his face. I can't stay here and listen to another word of this.

I drop down, grabbing my purse from the mess of bags and canvases at my feet, and turn to run back out into the rain.

"Betty! Wait!" Hayes pleads and I can hear him running after me but I don't stop.

It was a lie.

All of it was a lie.

And I'm the fool who fell for it.

Maybe I really do need a bodyguard.

Chapter Ten

H ayes

I've only been truly afraid twice in my life.

The first time was during the car accident that gave me this scar and killed my parents.

The second was turning around and seeing Betty looking devastated as I talked to her dad.

I deserve for her to run away from me, I know that I do after I betrayed her, but that doesn't stop me from chasing after her out into the rain.

"Betty, please!" I call as I jump down the front porch steps and into the mud in my socks.

I catch up to her, my hands going around her shoulders and spinning her so that she's facing me. There's rain dropping onto her face but I can still make out the tears streaming down between the raindrops and my heart breaks.

I did this to her.

"I'm an idiot," I mumble and she just stares at me. "I can explain though."

"Save it. I don't want to hear it," she says, her voice hard with anger and I hate it.

"Please, just hear me out," I beg her, my hands clasping between us and she glances down at them, her expression softening slightly.

When she glances back up at me though, her gaze is hard.

"I love you," I tell her and she looks away, anger radiating off of her in waves.

"No, you don't. You can't."

"I do," I argue but she shakes her head.

"Then I can't believe it."

"Betty," I start but she cuts me off.

"I can't believe that I bought all of this," she says, waving her hand at me standing in front of her pitifully. "When all along you were just doing your job."

"It's not like that."

"Sure, it is."

"Protecting you is the best job. One that I would gladly do, without pay, for the rest of my life."

She pauses at that and I rush to keep talking before she can get mad at me or try to leave again.

"I love you, Betty. I need you in my life. It's meaningless without you."

She stares at me, her green eyes searching my face, and I try to show just how much she means to me with a look. I'm sure that I don't pull it off. I've never been good at showing my feelings and Betty means too much.

"I know that you don't remember," I go on. "But the night that we met, you asked me to marry you."

She opens her mouth to say something, or maybe it just dropped open in shock. Either way, I press on.

"And I said yes."

"It was just the rum talking," she says but there's no force behind it.

Her eyes get this faraway look on it and I want to take her inside where it's not cold or wet, but I'm afraid to touch her right now.

"You know that it was more than that," I tell her and she glances up at me, looking uncertain. "You could feel it then too. Just like me. We're meant to be together."

She bites her full bottom lip as raindrops drip off the end of her nose and eyelashes.

"I love you, Betty. More than anything and I know that you deserve more than I could ever give you, but everything that I have is yours. It's all yours."

I hold my breath, hoping that I got through to her and that she won't leave. I don't know what I would do if she left me.

That's a lie. I do know. I would follow her around until one of us died.

"And my parents?" she asks hesitantly.

"They hired me that day in the parking lot and I know that I should have said no and told you about it, but I couldn't. I needed to be close to you, and I guess by your parents hiring me, it felt like I had permission to spend all of my time with you. I know that I'm not the most attractive guy," I start, my fingers going to the scar on my face and she grabs my hand.

"Yes, you are. Don't talk like that."

"I wanted to tell you a hundred different times, but I was afraid that you would be angry and leave me. I was trying to quit when you came in. I haven't been returning their calls or texts since they hired me and they were annoyed."

There's silence to that statement and I know that she's trying to decide if she can trust me after all of this. I hope that the answer is yes.

"I swear I was quitting, Betty. I never even got paid, so—"

"Shh," she hushes me and I shut up immediately.

She looks off toward the tree line and I fight the urge to pace as I wait to hear what the verdict is.

"Call them and quit right now," she tells me and it seems like a dare.

One that will be way too easy to complete.

I grab my phone out of my jean pocket and hit redial on their call. Ryan answers on the first ring, sounding panicked and I hold Betty's eyes as I start to speak.

"Is Betty okay?" he asks.

"Yes, but she knows."

"What?" he asks, sounding even more worried.

"And I quit."

He starts to say something, but I don't bother listening. I hold the phone out to Betty and she looks at the screen before she nods.

"I'll deal with them later."

I want to tell her that I get it. That she's the most precious thing in the world and I can understand why they want to make sure that she's protected at all times, but I know that it wouldn't be doing me any favors right now.

I hang up and slide the phone back into my pocket. I can feel it vibrating against my thigh and I'm sure that they're calling both of us repeatedly right now.

"So, it was real?" she asks hopefully and I nod.

"It was all real. I'm sorry that I didn't tell you. I'm sorry that I took the job in the first place. I shouldn't have."

She nods, weighing my words, and I try not to hold my breath as I wait for her to say something.

"And you love me?"

"More than anything."

She nods and I wonder if that's a good sign.

"That's good, because I love you too."

"You do?" I ask, my fingers clenching into a fist so that I don't grab her and pull her to me.

"Yeah. More than you'll ever know. That's why I was so upset when I found out about all of this," she says, waving her hand back toward the front door.

"So, you'll be mine?"

"I already am," she says with a sexy smile and I grin, reaching for her then.

My lips meet her wet ones and suddenly I don't care about the downpour happening around us. I've got my girl in my arms, her lips on mine, her hands in my hair, and her heart in my hands.

I'm determined not to do anything to jeopardize it again.

Chapter Eleven

B etty

One Year Later...

"I guess maybe the RV would have been a better idea," I say with a sigh as Hayes and I lay on our backs watching the top of the tent slowly bend toward our faces.

It's no match for the torrential downpour out there right now and I wonder if we should make a mad dash to his truck before it gets any worse.

Hayes is silently laughing beside me, and I roll over onto my side and prop my chin up onto his chest.

"Sorry that the vacation isn't going as well as we thought it would."

"Are you kidding me?" he asks with a grin, his blue eyes twinkling. "It's perfect."

I look back up at the ceiling which is hanging so low that I'm surprised the rods haven't snapped.

"Clearly," I say, doubt and skepticism dripping off every syllable.

Hayes is still chuckling but he pulls me closer.

"Every day with you is an adventure. My life before you was so boring that all of the days blend together. Now look at us."

I laugh as he throws one hand out and it bangs off the side of the tent.

"Should we go to the truck?"

"Yes, absolutely."

I help him gather up the sleeping bag, pillows, and lantern, and then he takes my hand and we sprint, laughing, through the rain and over to the truck. He holds the door open for me, letting me crawl in first and then he's hurrying in after me.

"I think I saw a hotel a few miles back," I say as he starts the truck and he nods, already getting ready to back out of the spot.

We're on our honeymoon. We got married six months ago but then one of my screenplays was picked up so we postponed our honeymoon. Then winter hit harder than we thought it would this year so it got pushed back even more. It's actually closer to our first wedding anniversary than our wedding day, but neither of us cares.

Hayes was in charge of planning our honeymoon and I had been so excited when he told me that we were going camping. I was a little surprised that he even remembered me mentioning that I wanted to camp and see Yellowstone, but I shouldn't have been. Hayes remembers everything that I say.

This trip isn't exactly going as we planned, but I don't

mind. I'm just glad to get to spend some quality time with my husband. We've both been so busy the last twelve months.

He started painting again and when we got married, he gave my parents one that they always admired as a wedding gift to them. When I asked why they got a gift, he told me that they had created the most perfect gift for him and he was just trying to repay it in some way.

My parents ended up posting the painting hanging in their house on Instagram and it blew up. Now Hayes is a successful painter with his first art gallery showing right around the corner.

As for me, my screenplay was picked up and made into a movie. It's set to release next month and I can't wait to go to opening night. I have another one in the works right now too and I have high hopes that someone will buy it too.

I ended up ignoring my parents for a few weeks but I knew that I couldn't cut them out of my life. Hayes helped me work through my feelings and shared his insights and I called them back about three weeks after everything happened.

I needed to forgive them and also invite them to our wedding. They had taken the news well and I'm assuming that I could have said anything and they would have been okay with it as long as I was talking to them again. Luckily for me, they adore Hayes and he loves them too.

Hayes pulls into the parking lot and then up to the door so that I don't have to run through the rain. All of our luggage is still in the back seat but we'll have to go back for the tent tomorrow though, as long as the rain has let up.

"You know what we should do," I ask as he comes around to get my door.

"What's that?"

"See if they have a honeymoon suite," I say as I wrap my arms around his neck and offer him my mouth.

He grins down at me before he presses his lips to mine and I smile back.

I can't wait to see all of the adventures we have together for the rest of our lives.

Starting with what we can get up to in the honeymoon suite tonight.

Chapter Twelve

H^{ayes}

Five Years Later...

"He's perfect," Ryan says as he looks down at his grandson.

I smile, agreeing with him one hundred percent. Betty is looking tired but happy as she watches her parents, son, and me from the hospital bed and I move closer to her side. When I brush some of her still damp hair away from her face, she turns and smiles softly up at me.

"You are amazing," I tell her and she turns her head, kissing the palm of my hand before she looks back at our son.

"Have you two decided on a name yet?" Emma asks as she moves to take her grandson from her husband.

"Not yet," I start but Betty stops me from going on.

"Actually, I was thinking about that," she says, biting her bottom lip as she starts to sit up a little more in the bed.

I move to help her, putting an extra pillow behind her back so she's more comfortable.

"How about Ben?" she says, her eyes studying my face as she says the name.

"Oh, after Hayes's father," Emma says, too busy staring down at our son to notice the look passing between Betty and me.

"Betty," I say, but I can't get any other words out.

"I think it's perfect," she says quietly, giving me that beautiful smile of hers.

I nod, tears threatening to spill from my eyes, and she reaches her hand out to me. I take it, this time kissing her palm and wrapping her fingers around the kiss.

Betty is the best thing that's ever happened to me, and I make sure that she knows it every day of our lives.

We've been married for five years now and with each year, each day that passes, I fall a little more in love with her. She was my entire world and now that our son is here, that world has just grown by one.

When Betty had told me that she was pregnant, it was a shock. We hadn't been trying necessarily, but the timing was perfect.

I had just finished up another gallery showing and she was about to dive into her latest project. We both decided to take some time to ourselves and try to enjoy the pregnancy and change to our lives.

The first order of business was to buy a bigger house. Our little cabin was great for the two of us, but there was no way that we could fit everything that a baby would need into it.

We still live in Redwood and Betty's parents even

bought the cabin next door to us. They are both retired now and they spend about half of their time with us and the rest traveling. I'm sure that now that Ben is here, that time will switch to mostly with us, but Betty and I are thrilled to have them close by in case we need anything.

"Do you need anything?" I ask her.

I know that visiting hours will be over soon and if she wants something to eat, I'd rather her parents were still here when I went out.

"About eight hours of sleep," she says with a half sigh, half laugh.

"We'll let you rest, honey. We'll be back with breakfast in the morning," Emma says as she passes me Ben.

He's sound asleep right now but I'm sure that he'll be hungry again soon. I'm hoping that Betty is able to sleep for a little bit before he wakes up again.

She was in labor for twenty-two hours and I was by her side for all of it. I wish that I could have done more, but she was a badass.

I watch as she hugs her parents goodbye and then she looks at me. Her eyes are half-mast and I lean down, kissing her forehead.

"Get some rest. I've got him," I promise her and she nods, her eyes finally drifting shut.

I start to rock with Ben in the chair by the window and I smile down at him.

"Let me tell you a story, son, about the most amazing woman in the world."

I smile as I start to tell him about the night that I met his mom. It was the best night of my life. It changed the whole course of my future and gave me my family.

And it was all thanks to too much rum.

About the Author

CONNECT WITH ME!

If you enjoyed this story, please consider leaving a review on Amazon or any other reader site or blog that you like. Don't forget to recommend it to your other reader friends.

If you want to chat with me, please consider joining my VIP list or connecting with me on one of my Social Media platforms. I love talking with each of my readers. Links below!

Website
Newsletter

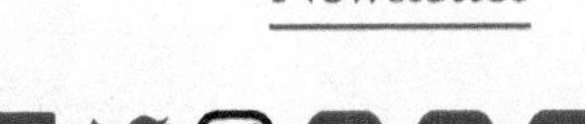

Series by Shaw Hart

Cherry Falls

803 Wishing Lane

1012 Curvy Way

Eye Candy Ink

Atlas

Mischa

Sam

Zeke

Nico

Eye Candy Ink: Second Generation

Ames

Harvey

Rooney

Gray

Ender

Banks

Fallen Peak

A Very Mountain Man Valentine's Day

A Very Mountain Shan Halloween

A Very Mountain Man Thanksgiving

A Very Mountain Man Christmas

A Very Mountain Man New Year

Folklore

Kidnapping His Forever

Claiming His Forever

Finding His Forever

Rescuing His Forever

Chasing His Forever

Folklore: The Complete Series

Holiday Hearts

Be Mine

Falling in Love

Holly Jolly Holidays

Love Notes

Signing Off With Love

Care Package Love

Wrong Number, Right Love

Kings Gym

Fighting Fire With Fire

Fighting Tooth and Nail

Fighting Back From Hell

Sequoia: Stud Farm

Branded

Bucked

Roped

Spurred

Sequoia: Fast Love Racing

Jump Start

Pit Stop

Home Stretch

Telltale Heart

Bought and Paid For

His Miracle

Pretty Girl

Telltale Hearts Boxset

Also by Shaw Hart

Still in the mood for Christmas books?

Stuffing Her Stocking, Mistletoe Kisses, Snowed in For Christmas, Coming Down Her Chimney

Love holiday books? Check out these!

For Better or Worse, Riding His Broomstick, Thankful for His FAKE Girlfriend, His New Year Resolution, Hop Stuff, Taming Her Beast, Hungry For Dash, His Firework

Looking for some OTT love stories?

Her Scottish Savior, Baby Mama, Tempted By My Roommate, Blame It On The Rum, Wild Ride, Always

Looking for a celebrity love story?

Bedroom Eyes, Seducing Archer, Finding Their Rhythm

In the mood for some young love books?

Study Dates, His Forever, My Girl

Some other books by Shaw:

The Billionaire's Bet, Her Guardian Angel, Falling Again, Stealing Her, Dreamboat, Making Her His, Trouble